P9-CKA-931

Bob Gill

The Present

chronicle books · san francisco

This is a story about a boy named Arthur.

One day, not too long ago, while he was looking for something in his dad's closet, Arthur noticed a package on the top shelf. It was wrapped in shiny paper with stars on it and tied with a bright red ribbon.

He almost hadn't noticed the package because it was partially hidden behind an old hat, a cardboard box, and a pair of hiking boots.

Arthur was sure it must be a surprise present for his birthday, which was just two weeks away. His mother always wrapped his presents with red ribbon.

Better an apple given than eaten. —*Anonymous*

Brooklyn-born Bob Gill's work as an artist and graphic designer
has spanned continents, and his genius has been stamped on a wide
range of creative endeavors, from children's books to Beatlemania.
He lives in New York City.

First published in the United States in 2010 by Chronicle Books LLC.
First Italian edition, *Il Regalo*, by Maurizio Corraini s.r.l. in February 2010.

Copyright © 2010 by Maurizio Corraini s.r.l.
Text and illustrations © 2010 by Bob Gill.

All rights reserved to Maurizio Corraini s.r.l. Mantova.
No part of this book may be reproduced in any form without
written permission from the publisher.

Library of Congress Cataloging-in-Publication Data available.
ISBN 978-0-8118-7743-5

Manufactured by Grafiche SiZ, Verona, Italy, in May 2010.

10 9 8 7 6 5 4 3 2 1

This product conforms to CPSIA 2008.

Chronicle Books LLC
680 Second Street
San Francisco, California 94107

www.chroniclekids.com

It must be a birthday cake, Arthur thought. You can't have a birthday without a birthday cake. He hoped it would be chocolate with lots of whipped cream.

Or maybe it was a ring toss. If he practiced a lot, he could become the world champion ring tosser and get his picture in the newspaper.

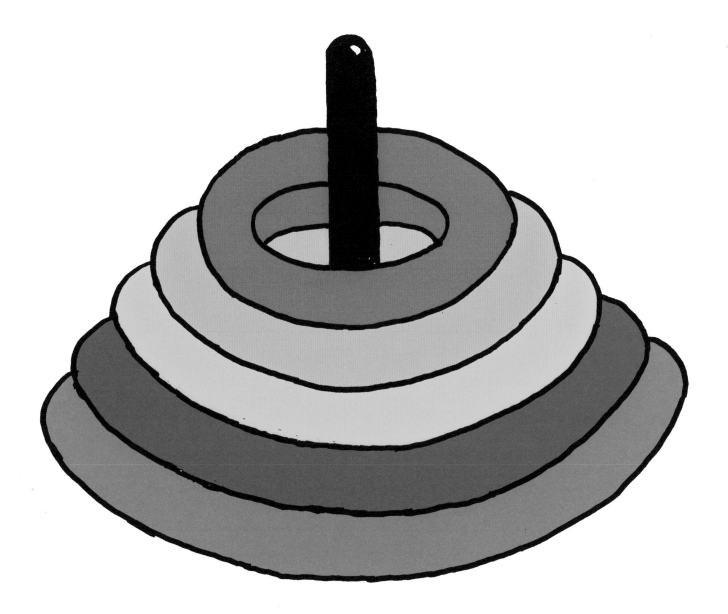

If the present were a sailboat, the first thing he would do would be to tie a string to it, take it to the pond in the park, and try to sail it.

If it were a tractor, he would hook it up to his friend's truck. They would pretend the truck had a flat tire, so the tractor could tow it to a garage.

What about a bowling set? No, the last thing he wanted was a bowling set. He hated bowling.

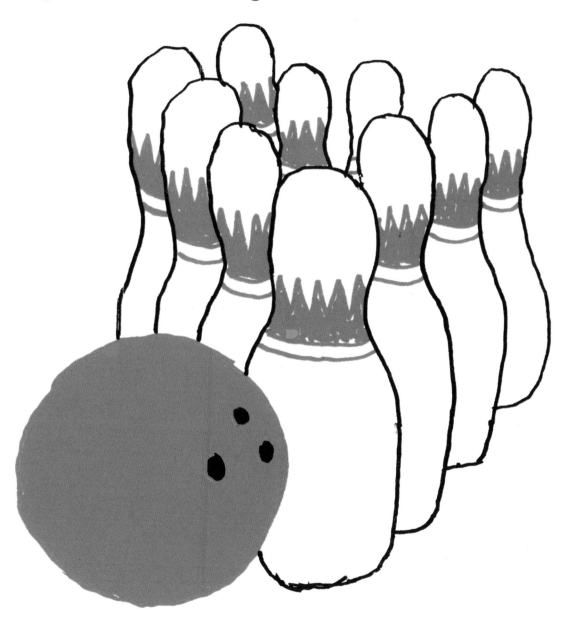

He'd prefer a really soft teddy bear.

Arthur's favorite candy was chocolate. How about a gazillion chocolate bars?

Gum balls wouldn't be so bad either.

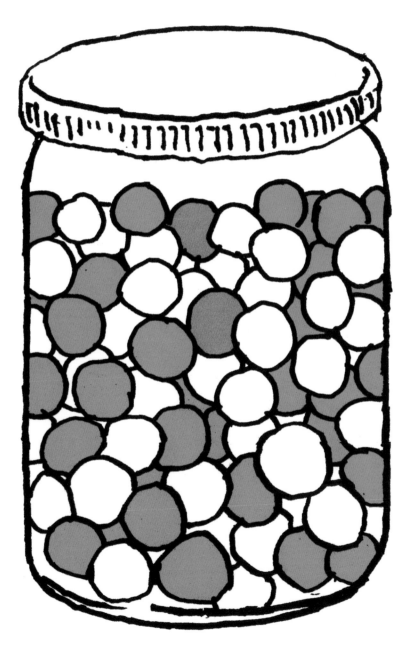

Arthur's backpack had a few holes in it. He was probably ready for a new one.

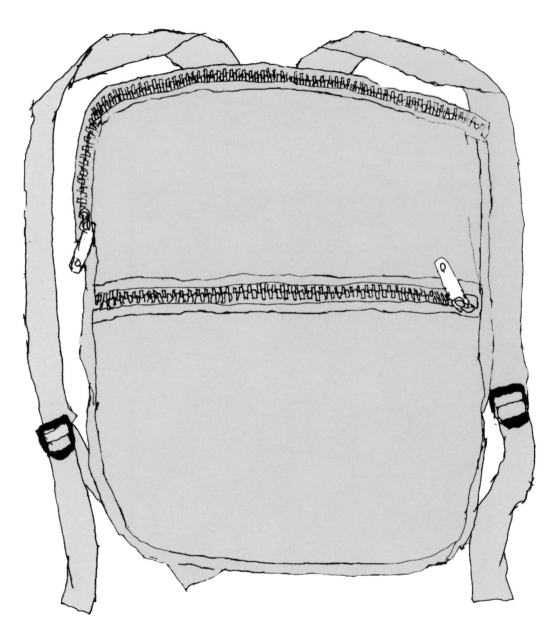

It might even be a Japanese lantern. He'd hang it over his bed, wondering what the Japanese writing meant.

If it were a paint box, he'd paint a picture of his house. And then he'd paint one of a tree, and then, after that, well, he wasn't sure what he'd paint.

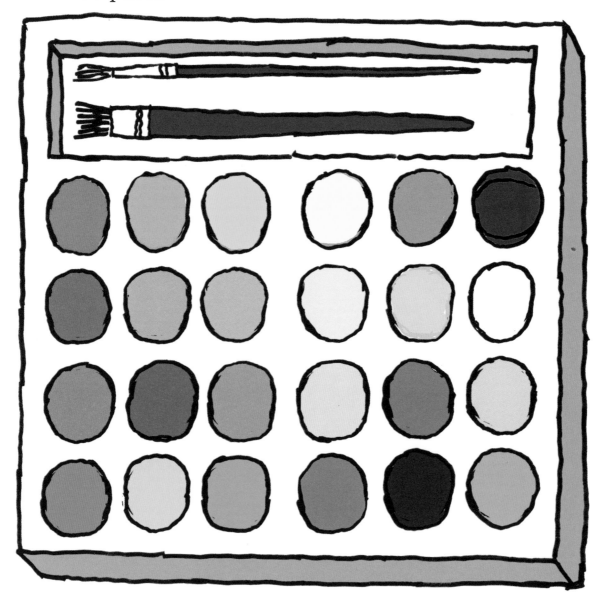

It might be a puzzle, but not one that was too easy—or too hard.

If the present were from Aunt Gert, it would be a scarf.
She gives a scarf every year.

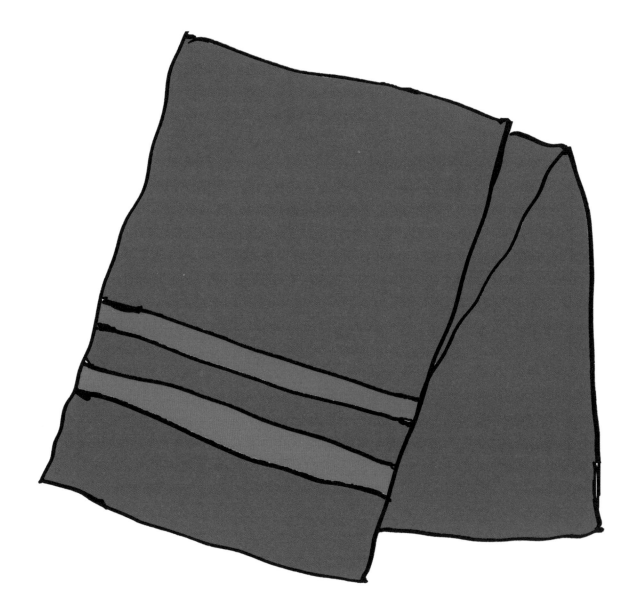

If the present were from Uncle Tony, it would be gloves.
He gives gloves every year.

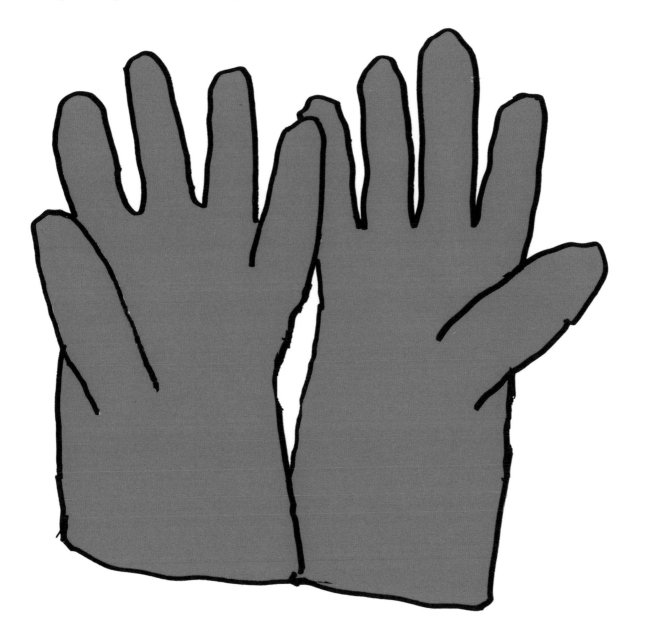

Arthur always wanted a kite. Maybe the present was a kite.

He had once asked for ice skates. Maybe he'd finally get them this birthday.

A TV wouldn't be bad. Lots of kids have their own TVs. Maybe he'd get one, too.

Or even a computer. A friend said he watched movies on his computer. That would be so cool.

Ever since he heard someone play a horn in a movie he saw,
he wanted to blow one just like it and make that strange sound.
What fun if the present were a horn.

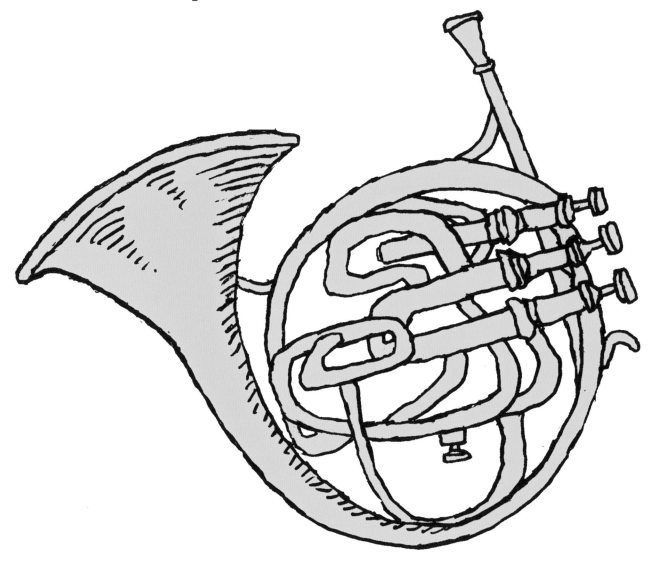

It could be a wheel. But he already had two wheels on his bicycle. He certainly didn't need another wheel.

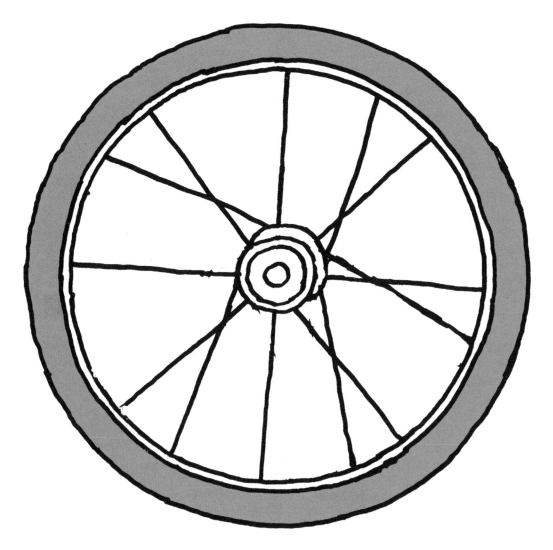

He wondered if it was a fish bowl with a fish swimming around.
No, it couldn't be a fish bowl: A fish wouldn't keep.

But it could be a dartboard like the one his cousin Harold had.

Since he knew how to tell time, he could really use a clock of his own.

But he would love to have a volleyball. Then maybe the big kids in the park would let him play with them.

Every day Arthur checked to make sure the present was still there.

Just when it seemed to Arthur that his birthday would never come, it was suddenly the day before the big day. He went to his dad's closet to look at the present one last time.

That's when the front doorbell rang. His mother answered the door. He heard her talking to a woman who said she was collecting toys for poor children.

Arthur climbed on the chair, got down the present, and ran over to where his mother and the woman were talking . . .

and he gave the woman the present.